SO-BNW-200

CATFISH CREEK

by
LOUISE PLISS

illustrated by
ANTHONY D'ADAMO

Reilly & Lee Co.   Chicago 1962

© Copyright 1962 by Reilly & Lee Co.
Manufactured in the United States of America
Library of Congress Catalog Card Number 62-16395

June 6, 1964

To Rita Ray.

Dont go! Stay awhile!

Affectionately

Louise Bliss

THE TRIP
DOWN CATFISH CREEK

THE
TRIP DOWN

to JESS *and* HY,

the parents of Jerry and Davy

Contents

THE TRIP
DOWN CATFISH CREEK

1

MARCUS MAKES A DEAL

Marcus opened one eye and watched the curtain fluttering saucily at his bedroom window. He opened the other eye and yawned, making an enormous animal-like noise. The birds were singing, the sun shining brightly, and a gentle breeze blowing.

It was the kind of day to make a boy jump out of bed joyously, ready to run down to eat a huge breakfast. But Marcus only blinked and said "Ugh." He raised one leg so that it was straight over his head and examined his toes. Again he said "Ugh" and lowered his leg. He started to crawl out of bed, changed his mind, and then hopped out the other side. This was the way

1

his day began, getting out of the wrong side of the bed.

Mechanically he brushed his teeth, splashed water in his face—this passed for washing—and then slowly put on his clothes.

Just as he was about to go downstairs, he met his mother in the hall. She was looking quite indignant.

"Marcus Cole," she said, "if I've told you once I've told you a hundred times that I don't want that turtle in the bathtub."

"But Boodle has to have some water. Where can I put it?"

"Put it in a pan of water and take it anywhere . . . anywhere where I won't step on it or touch it. I should think you'd be too big for things like that by now."

She looked at him despairingly for a moment and then went down to put his breakfast on the table. Slowly, he went into the bathroom, picked up his turtle, and held it up to see it in the mirror. He looked at his own red hair. It was standing up straight, like pieces of snipped yarn. He scowled and stuck his tongue out at himself.

Then he went downstairs and found an old pie tin, half-filled it with water, and tenderly set Boodle in it. As he sat down at the kitchen table he breathed deeply and the beginning of a smile passed over his face. There before him was a plate of steaming pancakes with lots of butter and a big jug of real maple syrup that his uncle had sent from Vermont. This was the first bright spot of the morning. Perhaps the day would not be so bad after all.

Then he heard his mother say, "Marcus Cole, if I've told you once, I've told you a hundred times that you can't eat with dirty hands."

"But I've just washed them." Marcus looked at his hands and couldn't imagine why she was saying such a thing. They looked more than usually clean to him.

Mrs. Cole turned them over and sure enough, there were streaks of dried mud. She sighed, probably wondering about the white linens she was so proud of and also wondering why boys always left dirty smudges on every towel they passed.

"Wash your hands!" she said crisply, and Marcus washed his dirty hands at the kitchen sink.

When he was finally ready to eat his pancakes, his mother sat beside him with her cup of coffee.

"Oh, by the way," she said pleasantly, "Dad asked me to remind you to finish weeding the tomatoes."

"Oh, no," he groaned. "This is supposed to be vacation and I have to work harder than schooltime."

"Oh, come now, it's not that bad. You're eleven years old. You ought to have some kind of responsibility."

Marcus's chin began to jut out the way it always did when he was angry. His face was peppered with freckles and his scowl made his eyebrows nearly meet over the bridge of his nose.

"Well, if I'm eleven, I ought to have some rights, too!"

"Why, Marcus, you have lots of rights."

"It's Marcus do this . . . and Marcus do that, just as if I was a baby instead of, well, instead of a human being."

"Why, Marcus . . . !"

"I'd like to have one day, just ONE day of being my own boss. Just one day of doing anything I want . . ."

Mrs. Cole looked surprised.

"Just one day . . ." He plunged his fork into the pancakes ferociously.

The surprise on his mother's face changed. It was now a curious look, as if some interesting thoughts were passing through her head.

"You know . . ." she began. "You know . . . ?" It was as if she were asking a question.

Marcus glanced at her suspiciously.

"You know, I think we just might be able to manage that!"

Marcus put his fork on the table and stared at her.

"All right," she went on, "you be your own boss for one day. You make your own decisions and do whatever you like. I won't interfere with anything you want to do, except, of course, if there's any danger."

"You MEAN that, Mom?"

"I mean it."

Then it was his face that had a curious look. He didn't quite believe that his mother meant it; and even if she did mean it, he wasn't quite sure that he liked it. But there she was, holding out her hand and asking him to shake on it.

"Is it a deal?" she asked.

"It's a deal."

Suddenly he yelled at the top of his voice and dashed upstairs. He ran over to the big toy chest in his bedroom and began to throw things out on the floor: balls, gloves, trains, trucks, bats, blocks, soldiers, and things that were so squashed they couldn't be identified. At last he came to a small box which he did not throw. He cradled it tenderly in the palm of his hand and opened it carefully. A smile spread over his face. He poked his finger into the box. What do you suppose was in it? A bit of dirt and some real live worms.

Now, it might seem that there wasn't a thing in the world that Marcus loved. But there was something that he loved and wasn't ashamed to admit it and that was animals. He didn't always have luck with them but that didn't keep him from bringing home anything he found that could crawl, wriggle, fly, swim, run, or jump. He once had a canary that escaped. His dog had died of old age miseries. His cat had been caught in a trap. Only the worms and Boodle, the turtle, remained. Boodle seemed to survive everything, including Marcus.

He wouldn't have to hide the worms today. By the terms of his deal he could do anything he liked. He put the box inside his shirt. He looked at his unmade bed, the toys scattered around the room. He knew that he should tidy up the room, that he really ought to pick up the toys. Pick up—don't pick up, pick up—don't pick up. "You make your own decisions . . ." his mother had said. Now this was a strange thing. If his mother had asked him to pick them up, he would have tried to get out of it; now that his mother wasn't telling him what to do, he felt like doing it. Pick up—don't pick up, pick up—don't pick up.

Slowly, thoughtfully, he approached the toy

chest. He picked up one tiny battered toy and flung it in quickly. That made him feel better. Then he picked up his pajamas and put them on the bed.

"I'm going over to Jerry's," he called over his shoulder to his mother. The moment he said it he realized that he didn't really have to tell her where he was going.

2

NOTHING SPECIAL TO DO

Marcus knocked impatiently on the back door of Jerry Stone's house and waited for an answer. Presently Mrs. Stone opened the door and said, "Why, Marcus, you're out early this morning. Won't you come in?"

Without answering, he brushed past her and went into the kitchen. "Hi, Jerry," he said, "let's go out to the barn."

"Hi, Marcus." Jerry was standing in the middle of the kitchen beside his little brother and they were both listening to their mother who was all dressed up in high heels and a hat and gloves.

"And don't forget to look for the Mexican basket," Mrs. Stone was saying.

"No, Mom."

"And don't forget to give the dog his biscuits."

"No, Mom."

"And don't forget to close the back door."

"No, Mom."

"Come on, Jerry," Marcus said. "Let's go."

Mrs. Stone glared at him and said, "Just a moment, young man."

She turned back to her boys and continued, "I guess that's all."

She stooped a little to kiss them. Jerry, who was nine, was at a boy's most unkissable age. He squirmed and twisted as if he were being bitten instead of kissed. Davy didn't mind being kissed. He was only six. But if Jerry felt that way about it, then Davy mustn't show that he liked it. That's the way it is with brothers.

"Have a good time on the bridge," Davy said with a smile, showing the gap where his front teeth used to be.

"Not ON the bridge," Jerry said.

"No, honey, it isn't that kind of bridge. This is a game that you play with cards."

"Oh, I understand." Davy really didn't understand. "But why is it called a bridge luncheon?"

"Boy!" Marcus whistled. "He doesn't know anything." He began to laugh while Davy's face turned pink.

"Marcus, you're being very rude." Mrs. Stone's voice was quite crisp. "Remember that you asked the same kind of questions when you were his age. No, Davy, a bridge luncheon is one where you have lunch and play bridge afterwards."

"Oh," replied Davy, "but you just had breakfast."

At this both Marcus and Jerry began to laugh.

Mrs. Stone said "Boys!" quite sharply. "You're absolutely right, Davy." Her voice became soft, "I've got some shopping to do and then I'm going to Mrs. White's early to help her fix things. Oh, by the way, here's Mrs. White's telephone number in case you need me."

"We don't need that," Jerry protested. It was dreadful, being treated like a baby in front of Marcus.

"You never know. After all, this is the first

11

time I've left you boys alone for a whole day."

"My mother leaves me alone," Marcus said. "In fact, today I'm going to be my own boss and do anything I want."

"That's very nice," replied Mrs. Stone, "but don't forget that you're a little older." She smiled at Marcus in a kindly way, wondering what had come over him lately. He never used to talk in such a boastful way.

Jerry looked at him, wishing that he could be just like him when he got older.

As soon as Mrs. Stone left, Marcus said, "Do you have to take him along?" He pointed to Davy.

"Yes," Jerry answered. "But don't worry about him. He won't get in our way."

"Honest, I won't get in the way," Davy said.

"Let's play in the barn." Marcus was already on the way out.

"Yes, let's play in the barn." Davy wanted to please the older boys.

The Stones's barn was enormous and full of wonderful things, such as little secret rooms, stalls where animals had once lived, piles of attractive junk, and cobwebs. The children liked to play there because they didn't have to pick things up or put things away or worry about being untidy.

The Stones's big airedale, Major, was already in the barn, resting on the cool cement floor. The boys wandered around the barn, upstairs and downstairs, in and out of the secret rooms. All of them being free for a day, they wanted to make some important decisions. But there was nothing in the barn that offered the making of decisions. They had always had freedom and had always made their own decisions in the barn, so today it held no extraordinary magic.

They found themselves wondering what to do. "I know," suggested Jerry. "Let's go fishing."

This was a game that Mrs. Stone had invented for them and ordinarily it was a great deal of fun for a long stretch of time. Since they lived so far from the lake and Catfish Creek wasn't good for anything, they pretended that the street was a river and they fished with poles made by tying pieces of rope to sticks and attaching clothespins to the rope.

They sat on the curb, which became the river bank. It was a dead-end street and they weren't threatened by passing traffic because there was no traffic. They threw their lines into the road and waited. Major came out of the barn and sat near them on the grass. He seemed to be watching over them. He was a dog who had learned not to be surprised by anything.

They caught all kinds of fish, fish that swam in the oceans and fish that swam in the seas, and fish that splashed around in sparkling brooks. Sometimes they caught clams and oysters, and sometimes they even found huge pearls in the oysters.

"Look at the pearls!" Jerry exclaimed, holding up a handful of shiny pebbles.

"Oh, can I have some?" Davy asked.

"Sure, it's your ocean as much as mine." He gave some pearls to Davy.

"Want some?" He held out his hand to Marcus.

"Naw. Those are just junky stones. I'm going to catch a whale." In a few moments he heaved and squirmed and shouted, "Look! I've got a whale. Help me get it in!"

Jerry and Davy dropped their poles and helped
Marcus. They all fell over backward on the grass.
To subdue the struggling whale they wrestled
and grunted, gasped and entwined their arms and
legs and laughed so hard that they nearly lost
the gigantic creature.

A lady passed by and scowled at them. "Don't
fight boys," she said. "Whatever you're fighting
about can be settled by talking it over."

"Oh, we're not fighting," Jerry wheezed, trying to be polite. "We've just caught a whale."

The lady looked surprised. She couldn't see anything that resembled a whale. Finally she went along, shrugging her shoulders and mumbling something under her breath.

Major, who had been watching them, must have decided that the game was getting too rough. He nuzzled the boys with his wet nose and after circling them, finally worked his way into the center of the group.

Marcus embraced Major and wrestled with him a while, then he said, "This is kid's stuff. Let's do something special."

"What's special?" Jerry asked.

Without answering Jerry's question, Marcus looked at Davy and asked, "Do you HAVE to have him tagging along?"

Davy's chin began to tremble but Jerry answered "Yes!" in such a way that Marcus knew he meant it. Marcus knew better than to plague Jerry where Davy was concerned, but he was glad that he didn't have a little brother to follow him around. The only thing that could be worse would be to have a little sister.

This recalled something to Marcus and he said, "Hey! Let's go over and get Clem."

Clem would do anything at all that he asked, without asking questions. Jerry would follow him only up to a point; then he would get stubborn. But Clem would follow him to the ends of the earth. What a pity it was that Clem was a girl.

"It's no fun over there," Jerry said. "That garage is too new and too clean. Let's . . ."

But Marcus was already on his way. So Jerry trailed after him, and Davy trailed after Jerry, and Major trailed after Davy.

3

THE *LILLYBELLE*

Clem Robie was rather lonesome that day. It was Wednesday, the day that her mother always went down to the drugstore to help. There weren't any girls to play with in the neighborhood and she couldn't play with the boys unless they asked her. Sometimes she wished that they would get a hundred new neighbors who had nothing but nine-year-old girls; sometimes she wished she were a boy so that she wouldn't have to give in every time they suggested anything.

At this moment Clem looked somewhat like a boy. She was thin and wiry and wore a shirt and blue jeans. The remarkable thing was her hair. She had tried to cut it herself to make it look like a boy's haircut. She had taken out huge chunks. Her mother, in despair, had taken her to the beauty parlor. The lady at the beauty parlor, in despair, had thrown up her hands and said, "I can't do a thing with it. We'll just have to wait until it grows some more."

Clem was now sitting on the sofa in the living room, twisting the short strands of hair around her fingers. As soon as her mother had left, with instructions as to where to find her lunch, Clem began to wander around the house and finally settled in front of the television set. It was a strange thing about houses. When you weren't alone in them, they were just there, surrounding you, protecting you. But when you were alone in them, the sounds became large and sharp; they rubbed and dripped and creaked. And the strangest sound was the sound of quietness.

Clem was listening. At last she turned on the television set and waited for it to do something. On one station there was a cartoon which she had seen many times. On another station there was an announcer, telling her to smoke cigars.

19

She laughed and pretended to blow smoke rings. She turned a knob and there was another announcer, telling her to buy an automobile. Finally there was a lady behind a great pile of soapsuds, smiling because she was so happy to be doing the dishes.

"Ugh," thought Clem, "this is boring. How can anyone be so happy doing dishes?"

She liked to use the word "boring." Sometimes she used it when she was really bored; sometimes she used it because she couldn't think of anything else to say.

Now she was really bored. She turned the knob again and watched the squiggly little lines. Then she turned it off altogether and watched the tiny cube of light linger on the screen. This was the best part of television.

She was so lonesome that she felt like crying. Here it was summer and the weather was beautiful but what good was it if you didn't have anyone to talk to or play with! Everything was the same, day after day. Nothing ever changed.

Suddenly Clem caught a glimpse of the boys

coming toward her house. She jumped up and ran to the window, being very careful not to be seen through the curtains. Marcus, as usual, was first and there were Jerry, Davy, and Major close behind.

She felt a flutter of excitement as she jumped from window to window to keep them within her sight. Not only did she want to be a boy but she wanted to be a boy like Marcus. He was so big and didn't seem to be afraid of anything. It was true that he was sometimes rude and rough and boastful but he was never boring and that was very important.

There they were, coming right into her yard, going back toward the garage. She closed her eyes and wished hard that they would stay and play in her yard. She wished so hard that her eyelids hurt. But the thing that she mustn't, mustn't do, was to let them know how she felt.

Clem heard the knock at the back door. She stood behind the screen and said, "Hello."

"Come on out," said Marcus.

"Why?" she asked.

"We're going to do something."

"What?"

"I don't know. Just something."

"I'm kind of busy," Clem said.

"Okay," Marcus shrugged. He turned around.

"Ah . . . just a minute," she said, feeling a little panic in her stomach. "Maybe I can come out for a little while."

She went out, carefully closing the screen door, just to let them know that she was in no special hurry to join them.

"What happened to your hair?" asked Jerry. "You look scalped."

"Oh, I just had it cut short. It's cooler that way."

"Looks good," Marcus said. "Can we play in your garage?"

"Sure, my father won't care."

They went out to the garage and sat down on the floor crosslegged. There wasn't very much to look at, nor was there very much to say.

"Pretty small," said Jerry, with a touch of scorn in his voice. "Only holds one car. Our barn holds two cars and a little truck."

"Isn't supposed to be big," answered Clem.

"What's that?" asked Marcus. He pointed to a bulky form set on two sawhorses and covered with a tarpaulin.

"I don't know," Clem replied.

"Well, let's go," said Marcus. "Nothing to do here."

"Yeah, let's go," Davy agreed. He was beginning to think that it wasn't very interesting to play with bigger children. He wanted some action.

Clem gulped. What could she do to keep them? Or at least, what could she say to make them ask her to go with them?

"What's that in your shirt?" she asked.

Marcus suddenly remembered the box of worms. Hurriedly he pulled the box out of his shirt, hoping that the worms hadn't been squashed while they were landing the whale.

He dumped the dirt on to the floor and they watched the squiggly little creatures crawl around, making their soft bodies go in peculiar coiling movements.

"Why don't they go in a straight line?" Clem

23

asked. She hoped that Marcus wouldn't ask her to hold one.

Marcus ignored her question, as usual, and picked up a large worm. Clem moved back. "Want to hold it?" he offered.

"I do," said Jerry bravely. He picked up the worm and let it dangle on his forefinger.

"Now me," said Davy.

Marcus dropped a worm in the palm of his hand and Davy dropped it immediately because it tickled.

"Here." Marcus held the worm out to Clem. She shouted "No!" with such violence that Marcus thought it wouldn't be good for the worm to let her hold it.

Then Marcus gathered his worms, replaced them in the box, and put them back in his shirt.

"Let's go," he said.

"Yes, let's go," Jerry repeated. "Major!" He whistled and Major came out of his shady hole behind the garage.

Clem stood perfectly motionless. She tried desperately hard to think of some way of keeping them there, but her mind became frozen. Her mouth tightened and she kicked at a tiny ridge of cement until her toe hurt.

"I don't care," she said. "I'm kind of busy, anyway."

"Where's Davy?" Jerry asked.

"How do I know? I've got more things to do than keep track of him." Marcus hitched up his jeans and surveyed the neighboring houses.

"Hey! Davy!" Jerry called.

"I'm back here." Davy's voice came from behind the tarpaulin-covered object in the back of the garage. "Come here. Look at this." He was holding the tarpaulin out and trying to peer under it.

"What is it?" Jerry asked. He went back and put his head under the tarpaulin along with Davy's and suddenly cried, "It's a boat!"

Marcus looked interested and Clem looked startled.

"Where did this come from?" Marcus asked.

"I don't know," Clem answered.

They walked around the object several times

and then Marcus asked, "Can we pull off the cover?"

"Sure," Clem said. "My father won't care." Her mind was becoming unfrozen.

They pulled off the cover and there was a small canoe, sitting upside down on two sawhorses. There were some letters printed on it but since they were upside down, the children had to get down on their knees and become upside down too, in order to read them.

"L-I-L-L-Y-B-E-L-L-E," Marcus spelled. *"Lillybelle.* What a crazy name for a boat."

"I think I remember now." A light began to spread over Clem's face. "A man gave it to my father once . . . when we were down to the lake. I remember . . ."

"It's real keen," Jerry said, with admiration.

"It's keen," Davy echoed.

"Hey, Clem, can we play with it?" Marcus asked.

"Sure," Clem replied, "My father won't care." The lump had disappeared from her chest, the

tight mouth was relaxed, and a glow of pleasure spread over her face. "I really had some important things to do, but I guess they can wait."

4

BOATS CAN GO ANYWHERE

For a few minutes the children walked around the *Lillybelle*, feeling the surface and getting accustomed to the wonder of finding a real boat in a garage.

Presently Jerry said, "How can we play with it if it's up on those things?"

"Get it down," Marcus said, simply.

Clem looked somewhat doubtful but she knew that she had to choose between being alone and doing as Marcus said.

"Sure, get it down," she directed with a wave of her hand.

They explored the possibilities of getting it

29

down by trying to lift the rim off the sawhorses. It was surprising how light it was.

"Why, it's only canvas." Jerry exclaimed.

"Of course," Marcus said scornfully. "What did you think?"

Carefully, they lifted the canoe off the sawhorses and set it down on the floor. Then they picked it up and set it out on the lawn.

The *Lillybelle* was dusty from years of storage but it looked beautiful to the children. Clem was immensely happy to discover that she was the daughter of the owner of a real boat. And the boys were happy because at last they had found something special to do. Even Major was happy because he discovered that he could lie in the shadow of the canoe and still be near the children.

They ran their fingers over the long, slightly curved rail of the sides of the canoe and along the crossbars and over the ribs that shaped it.

Then, without asking permission, Marcus climbed in and sat on the crossbar. The others followed. Davy sat on the other crossbar. Jerry sat in the bow and Clem had no choice but to sit in the stern. They sat silently, staring straight ahead into nothingness.

Major soon became curious and climbed in, but he wouldn't sit still so they pushed him out again.

"You're rocking the boat," Jerry scolded. This seemed very funny, to rock a boat on green grass, so they laughed and this brought them up sharply to the business of how to play in a canoe on dry land.

"Let's go on a voyage," Jerry suggested.

"Yes, let's go on a voyage," Davy echoed. Then he added, "What's a voyage?"

"A trip," Jerry explained, "on water."

"But we're on grass."

"Bro-ther!" Marcus snapped.

"We're just pretending, Davy," Clem said, gently.

"Where'll we go?" Jerry asked.

"To Africa," Clem replied.

"No," Marcus disagreed hotly. "We're going to Japan."

"Africa!"

"Japan!"

"Africa! It's MY boat."

"What difference does it make," said Jerry. "Boats can go anywhere."

Marcus finally agreed that they would go to Africa, not because he wanted to be agreeable, but because he wanted to be the captain. In fact, he had already made up his mind that, as the oldest, it was proper that he be the captain and he didn't want a mutiny on his hands so soon.

"All right," he said, "we'll go to Africa. Now! Who's going to be the captain?"

"Oh, you are," exclaimed Clem. "You're the oldest, so you should be the captain."

"Okay with you, Jerry?" Marcus asked.

"Okay." Jerry wasn't very interested in rank. He was still exploring the structure of the canoe.

"Okay, Davy?"

"Okay." Davy was a little surprised that he should be consulted. Pleased, he added, "It's okay with Major, too."

Since Marcus was now officially the captain, it was agreed that he should sit in the stern to keep his eyes on things and to give orders. So they all got out, reshuffled their positions, and got in again. Now, with Marcus in the stern, Jerry was in the bow and Davy and Clem sat on the crossbars. They were ready to depart.

"Wait a minute!" cried Jerry. "The paddles! We forgot the paddles!"

He and Clem went back to the garage and in a few minutes they found the paddles. They were standing in a corner, mixed with several poles. He gave one to Clem and he kept the other.

It took them a while to learn that they couldn't both paddle on the same side of the boat. Their paddles kept clicking against each other. When this problem was solved, they had to learn to keep from tearing up the grass with them. By the longest stretch of her imagination Clem couldn't believe that her father "wouldn't care" about having his precious lawn ruined.

At last Marcus barked, "Lift anchor!" and they were off to sea. Major curled up in the shade of a horse chestnut tree and watched them. It is difficult to know if a dog can show amusement, but if he could, Major was a dog showing it at that moment.

Clem and Jerry were now paddling smoothly. The sky was blue, the sun was hot, and it was a lovely day for a voyage, even if there wasn't any water.

After a few minutes Jerry cried, "I see Africa!"

"Where?" the others shouted.

"Over there." Jerry pointed to the horse chestnut tree.

Marcus made binoculars by curling his fingers around his eyes.

"Oh, yes, I see," he said.

"Now I think I see a camel." Jerry pointed to Major who was dreaming and snapping at flies at the same time.

"Prepare to land!" Marcus ordered. "Davy, you be in charge of weapons. Gather all the weapons in case the natives attack us."

"Okay. But what kind of weapons?"

Marcus lost his dignity and yelled, "How can we play with him? He doesn't know anything. He's too little."

"You know what weapons are, Davy," Jerry said. "Like guns and tanks and cannons."

"Of course I know," said Davy. "He just thinks he's too smart. I'll get some weapons a'right. I'll get some guns and tanks and bows and arrows and pop-guns and everything." Angrily, he picked up the weapons from the bottom of the boat, from the air, from the water, and stuffed them into his pockets.

Clem began to feel uncomfortable. She hated to have Marcus talk to Davy that way. But she was afraid to say anything to him.

"Clem, you take care of food supplies," Marcus roared.

"Yes, sir."

"Pack some supplies to take along in case we're cut off."

"Yes, sir." Clem didn't like the way Marcus was shouting at them. He was taking the game much too seriously. He even looked as if he enjoyed shouting. She picked up an imaginary box and filled it with sandwiches, milk, and a big bottle of vitamin pills.

"Someone will have to swim ashore and be an advance scout to see if it's safe for us to land." Marcus looked at the others with a challenge in his eye.

"I'll volunteer, sir," Jerry said. He put the paddle in the bottom of the boat, put on his skin-diving gear, and dipped his hand in the water to feel the temperature. It was just right. Then he put his fingertips together and made a beautiful swan dive. He spread his body on the grass, face downward, and flayed his arms in a swimming stroke. When he reached shore, he signalled that all was safe, and the *Lillybelle* was anchored under the hot Egyptian sun.

The crew left the boat and crept stealthily up to the chestnut tree. They waited and listened. It was very quiet.

"Are we in Africa?" Davy shattered the silence.

"SHHHHH!" they all turned on him.

He thought that they were being silly so he began to stroke Major.

They turned on him again. "Don't do that! That's a camel!"

36

"What are we going to do in Africa?" Davy was willing to go anywhere if he only knew what he was supposed to do.

"We're going to see the pyramids," Clem whispered.

"What are pyramids?"

"They're . . . sort of things . . . like this." She made a triangle out of her arms. "They're big at the bottom and little on top."

"Oh," said Davy, confused. He was losing interest in the whole voyage idea. He wandered off, deciding to play by himself. He wished that his mother would come home.

"Come back here!" Marcus croaked in a loud, hoarse whisper. "Do you want to get attacked?"

"Yes, I do," said Davy, " 'cause I'm hungry. I want to go home and I want to see my mother and I'm hungry."

"Oh, Davy." Clem put her arm around him sympathetically. "Come to think of it, I'm hungry too."

"I am, too," said Jerry.

Marcus looked rather collapsed. He could see

that his crew had gone to pieces and was in no mood to be put back together again.

He had some fast thinking to do. He liked playing this game where he gave all the orders and had to take none. There must be some way of making it continue. Ah! He had it. He remembered the deal that he had made with his mother; and he remembered that Mrs. Stone would be gone for the day and that Mrs. Robie always went down to the drugstore on Wednesday.

"Let's have a picnic," he suggested. "How about it? Everyone can go home and get some food and then we can put it all together on the boat."

"Hey, that's a keen idea," Jerry said.

Clem looked at Marcus with admiration and sighed, "Oh, Marcus, how do you ever think of so many things?" Because of Marcus, the boys would probably stay in her yard for the whole afternoon.

Davy didn't care where he ate, as long as he

ate. And now that they were speaking of food, he forgave Marcus for all the mean things he had said.

5

PICNIC

"See you back here in fifteen minutes!" Marcus called over his shoulder as he ran home to get his lunch.

"Ten minutes!" called Jerry.

"Five minutes!" called Clem, but the boys had already gone and she was saying it to herself.

The first thing that Clem did when she went into the house was to telephone her mother.

"Mom," she told her mother, almost in one breath, "the boys are playing in our yard and we're playing in that old boat of Daddy's in the garage and we're going to Africa in it and I'm having more fun than I've ever had in my whole life."

Mrs. Robie was delighted. Clem hadn't been this excited in a long time. To think that the children would have fun in that funny little canoe . . . what was its name? Oh, yes, the *Lillybelle*. She remembered when the man who had the cottage next to theirs at the lake had given it to her husband. He hadn't known what he was to do with it, but he had been very pleased to receive it. There was no water near Chestnut Valley, except Catfish Creek, and goodness, that wasn't good for anything. What lovely imaginations children had! To think of their making a toy of a canoe on dry land!

"Mom, can I pack my lunch in a box?"

"Of course, dear. There are some boxes up in the cupboard. Have a good time. And," she added with a chuckle, "don't get wet."

Clem found her lunch, wrapped in colorful paper and little pieces of ribbon, just where she always found it in the refrigerator. She hoped that the boys wouldn't laugh because it was so fancy. Well, if they did, she didn't care. Suddenly, she found herself feeling quite brave, so brave, in fact, that she added some dainty pink and white napkins.

In the meantime, Jerry and Davy looked into their refrigerator and saw a dazzling assortment of good things to eat. There was cold meat, peanut butter and jelly, cheese, a pitcher of lemonade, and homemade cookies. Mom had even remembered to leave the butter out on the table. Everyone knows that trying to spread hard butter is the most exasperating thing in the world.

They put everything out on the table, made some sandwiches, and wrapped it all in yards and yards of waxed paper. Then, when they looked for something in which to carry the array, they remembered the Mexican basket. That was what they usually used for picnics.

"Where do you suppose it could have gone?" Jerry asked aloud, even though he knew that his question would not be answered.

"I dunno," Davy shrugged, just as he had shrugged many times before when questioned about it.

"Well," Jerry decided, "we haven't got time to look for it now, have we?"

"No," Davy agreed, "we're too busy."

Just as they were about to leave, the telephone rang. It was Mrs. Stone, checking on them.

"We're going to have a picnic, Mom. Is that all right?" Jerry sounded quite excited.

"Sure, that's fine," she answered. She was relieved to learn that they weren't moping around waiting for her to come home. "Let me say 'hello' to Davy."

"Hi, Mom," Davy said.

"Hi, Davy, are you having fun?"

"Oh, boy," he shouted so loud that Mrs. Stone had to remove the receiver from her ear, "we sure are. We're going to Africa in Clem's boat."

"In her WHAT?"

Jerry took the telephone from Davy and explained, "We found an old boat out in Clem's garage and we're playing in it."

"Does Mrs. Robie know about it?"

"Oh, Clem says that her father doesn't care. We can't hurt it or anything . . ."

"Very well," she said and added, laughing, "don't get seasick."

When Marcus went home to get his lunch,

he found his mother in the kitchen, ironing.

"Hi!"

"Hi, Marcus."

Marcus looked into the refrigerator and mumbled to himself. He opened it, shut it, opened it again, as if he weren't quite sure where to begin. Then he brought several things out and spread them on the table. He tried to whistle. He couldn't get anything to come out of his mouth so he hummed instead.

First there were some slices of bread. He didn't see anything that would make a man-size filling so he took a bowl of cold mashed potatoes. He spread the mashed potatoes between slices of bread. Some of it spilled on the floor. He picked it up and continued to spread it. Then he sprinkled it generously with pepper and garlic salt, which he thought to be ordinary salt.

Poor Mrs. Cole didn't have the heart to watch him. She thought that as a parent she shouldn't allow him to eat that mess. But a deal was a deal and she managed to keep quiet.

After the sandwiches were ready and packed

in a shoebox, he looked for something else. A drink was necessary, especially if they were going to Africa. He found a bottle of grape pop and poured it into a big pitcher. It didn't look like very much so he squeezed some oranges and lemons and added some water. Testing the mixture, he made a horrible face, but much to his mother's surprise, he said, "Ah, good!" and smacked his lips.

He grasped the handle of the pitcher with such force that his knuckles stood out like little marbles and he scooped up the box of sandwiches.

"G'bye."

"Good-bye, Marcus."

"We're going on a trip."

"That's nice. Will you be home for dinner?"

"I guess we'll be back in time. We're going to Africa in Clem's boat."

Mrs. Cole looked startled. She coughed and almost burned a hole in a white shirt.

"Have a good time," she said, "and watch out for sharks."

When the children returned to the *Lillybelle,*

they found that they had gathered enough food to last for a real trip to Africa. There were so many lunches, so much paper, so much string, so many boxes, so many paper plates, so many arms, legs, and knees that there wasn't enough room in the *Lillybelle* to hold it all. They had to spread everything on the lawn, under the hot African sky.

Marcus looked at the other lunches and then looked at his own. Something was wrong. He should have asked his mother to fix his, even though they had a deal. Hungry as he was, his own sandwiches looked like lumps of modelling clay.

"Say," he said to Clem, "those are pretty nice looking sandwiches you have. Did you make them yourself?"

"Oh, no, my mother fixed them."

"Peanut butter?"

"Uh-uh, ham and cheese, and let me see," she munched and examined the contents of her packages. "And cream cheese and jelly."

"Oh, boy," he said.

"Want one?" she asked.

"Thanks a million." He took one of her sand-wiches and pushed his own away.

"Want some cookies, Marcus?" Jerry asked.

"Gee, thanks ever so much." He took a fistful from the box that Jerry held out and gobbled them greedily.

Major began to sniff at the mashed potato sand-wiches. Marcus held some of the potato in his hand and fed him.

"We're not supposed to feed Major at the table," Davy said.

"But there isn't any table," Marcus laughed.

Marcus was right. So Major received more than his share of handouts and several things that were not handed out.

The children ate with dirty hands and talked with their mouths full. This was the best picnic that they had ever had. The very best.

6

BOATS ARE SUPPOSED TO MOVE

After lunch there was a short lull during which the children lay on their backs in the grass and gazed up at the sky. It was hot and they were full. Davy fell asleep for a few minutes, but the others watched the branches of the horse chestnut tree move ever so slightly against the blue. It was so quiet, as if they were daydreaming and didn't want to disturb their dreams with speaking. It looked so peaceful, so very peaceful.

Then, Marcus, with a shout, jumped up and cried, "Let's get going!" It was like an alarm going off in the middle of the night.

"Where we going?" Davy asked. His small nap had given him enough energy to WALK to Africa.

48

Marcus ignored him as usual and bellowed, "Get back to your posts. We're ready to start."

"But where are we now?" asked Clem.

"Anywhere," he answered. "It doesn't matter."

"I thought we were still in Africa," said Jerry.

"Then let's go to China. We'll go around the Indian Ocean." Marcus had already taken his position in the stern and the others scrambled in after him.

Jerry and Clem began to paddle. During the first few minutes they paddled so fast that you would have thought that they needed to arrive in China by sunset. But gradually they slowed down until they were scarcely moving at all.

Davy stood up in the boat and stretched.

"Sit down, small fry!" Marcus commanded.

"I don't like this game anymore," Davy complained. "It's too sitting."

Clem leaned forward and whispered to him, "Sit down, little Davy. We'll move around pretty soon." To tell you the truth she was getting bored with sitting too, but she was afraid that the boys

49

would leave her, if the boat game was finished.

So they sailed on, with Marcus giving orders and scanning the horizon with his finger binoculars. "Now we're going along the west coast of Africa. Now we're sailing around the Cape of Good Hope. Now we're in the Indian Ocean."

No one dared to suggest that they play another game as long as Marcus was having a good time.

Finally Jerry put down his paddle, stood up, and announced, "I've had enough of this. Boats are supposed to move!"

"Hooray, let's move!" Davy looked up, relieved and full of pride in his brother's courage.

In a way Clem was glad that it was Jerry who had broken the silence and yet she was afraid that it would mean the end of the afternoon.

Marcus was thinking. They all waited for him to speak.

At last he said, "Do you–you really want to move?"

"Sure!"

"And how!"

"But how can we?"

"Well," he said, "do you see that red wagon in the garage?"

Their heads moved in unison and they looked at Clem's red wagon and still wondered what that had to do with the *Lillybelle*.

"We'll put the boat on it and pull it!"

There was a short silence during which they considered his words. Marcus was looking at them as if he dared them to disagree with him.

"My father won't care," Clem said, timidly.

"You know, that's a keen idea," Jerry seemed to be thinking about the possibilities.

Before they had a chance to accept the idea fully, Marcus had already pulled out the wagon. The boat was very light. It would be easy to lift it.

"Pick it up," he ordered. "Jerry, you pick up the other end and Clem, you get in the middle."

Mechanically, they obeyed his orders and soon they had the *Lillybelle* perched on the wagon, as neat as you please.

"I'll take the first ride," Marcus announced, "just to make sure it's safe." He began to climb in but found that it was almost impossible without pulling the boat off the wagon. The weight of his pulling himself up was too much for the frail little craft.

"We need steps," Jerry said.

Steps. Steps. What could they use for steps?

"I know. I've got it," said Clem excitedly. "Wait! Don't go away."

She disappeared into the house and returned with her mother's little two-step ladder that was used for cleaning high places. That was perfect! Marcus stepped into the *Lillybelle* like a king stepping into his carriage.

"All right! Now pull!" he ordered.

Clem and Jerry reached for the wagon handle but found that the boat extended out so far that they couldn't get hold of it unless they crawled under the bow. And, of course, if they were under the bow, they couldn't pull.

"Now what?" Clem asked. It was very discouraging but it was still better than being alone.

"Let me think," Marcus said from his lofty position.

"Let's move," Davy begged. Major came out of his cool hole and stood beside him.

"Shut up!" Marcus shouted. "Can't you see I'm thinking?"

Jerry and Clem walked round and round the wagon, as if, by doing that, they would find the solution for their problem.

"I've got it!" Marcus shouted, at last. "A rope! Get a rope!"

There wasn't any rope in the Robie garage. In fact, there was nothing in the Robie garage, now that the *Lillybelle* and the little red wagon were out of it.

Jerry ran home to his barn. He knew that whatever they might need, he would be able to find it in the old barn. Soon he returned with a long piece of thick worn rope. He and Clem crawled under the boat and looped it through the handle right in the rope's middle. They knotted it once, to keep it from slipping. Then they crawled out again, each with an end of the rope. Then they tried pulling. It worked.

Marcus settled back and folded his arms. Jerry

and Clem pulled the end of the frayed rope and Davy and Major trailed along behind. Davy wondered why in the world anyone would think that this was fun.

Thus began the first leg of a remarkable voyage.

7

BOATS ARE FOR WATER

Marcus was having the time of his life, perched up on the *Lillybelle,* giving orders, surveying the familiar neighborhood landscape, and shouting, "Ahoy! ahoy!" from time to time.

Jerry and Clem were not sure that they were having a good time. It was difficult pulling the wagon. It kept swaying from side to side and the rope was beginning to cut into their hands. The sidewalk was broken in places and they had to be careful about spilling their passenger.

Davy was sure that he was not having a good time. He and Major made a sorry sight, trailing behind, expecting never to get a turn at riding.

In the meantime, they were so concerned about

making the boat move that they scarcely noticed the other children of the neighborhood gathering around them. There was one big boy, about Marcus's age, and several small children, about Davy's age. They were admiring the real boat and the neat way in which it was made to move. And, naturally, it wasn't long before they began to ask for rides.

At first they were refused outright. No one was going to ride in their own special private boat.

"Go get your own boat!" Marcus said, knowing full well that there wasn't another boat in the whole village of Chestnut Valley.

Finally, the big boy said, "I'll give you a penny for a ride."

Marcus looked down at him. There was a gleam in his eye.

"We'll think about it," he said.

He tried to get down but couldn't without the step ladder. They had left the ladder back in Clem's yard. Marcus ordered Clem to go back and get it. Without a word she dropped the rope and fetched the ladder and Marcus was helped to the ground. Then they held a conference about selling rides.

"Sounds all right to me," Jerry said.

"Sounds all right to me," Davy echoed. He wasn't sure what was happening but anything that was all right with Jerry was all right with him.

"I don't know. I don't think it's right," said Clem, running her hands through her chopped-off hair.

"Why not?" Marcus asked, impatiently.

"Just because . . ." Clem replied.

"There you go!" Marcus barked. "What kind of an answer is that, 'just because'?"

"Because it's selfish," Clem blurted, almost in tears to have Marcus raise his voice.

Marcus sighed, wishing that there could be a world without girls. Yet, he hadn't forgotten that it was her boat. There was one thing that he had learned about Clem. You could push her, it was true; but could push her only so far

far and then she could get stubborn as a mule. He was having a lot of fun with the silly little boat and he didn't want it to end yet, so he decided to compromise.

"How about charging a penny a ride and giving the money to a worthy cause?"

"What worthy cause?" she asked, suspiciously.

"How about the Red Cross?"

"Okay," she agreed.

"Okay, Jerry?"

"Okay," said Jerry.

"Okay," echoed Davy.

Marcus was about to say that he didn't count, but he decided to be careful until they were over this delicate spot.

"The rides are a penny, up and down the street once," Marcus announced. "Who's got a penny?"

The children looked around at each other rather timidly and three of them raised up their pennies.

"That's not much to give to the Red Cross . . . three pennies," Jerry said.

"Maybe we can start with this and drum up more business later," Marcus insisted.

"Maybe they can get some pennies," Clem suggested.

"Who can get pennies from your parents?" Marcus asked.

Three more hands went up.

"Hmph! Six cents for the Red Cross," Jerry said.

"Maybe this is just the beginning," Marcus assured him. "Here you are." He beckoned the big boy toward the boat. He held the step ladder firmly and the big boy climbed in and waited for action.

There wasn't very much action. Not a penny's worth anyway. It looked exciting from the ground but the boat moved so slowly and swayed so much that he stopped them and insisted on getting back his penny.

The next customer was a tiny little girl who looked frightened even before she approached the *Lillybelle*. Marcus took her penny and Jerry and Clem lifted her up to the boat. She held the sides, which she could hardly reach, and waited grimly. As soon as the wagon began to move she let out a long, wailing howl of fright that rang out through the neighborhood.

"Lemme OUT, lemmme out, lemmmme out! You're trying to KILL me!"

The *Lillybelle* swayed and almost tipped off the wagon. Marcus stopped it and lifted her down, rather roughly. She sobbed and ran home as fast as she could.

"It's a gyp," the big boy growled.

"It's not our fault that she was a fraidy-cat," Marcus protested.

The spectators, instead of gathering around the *Lillybelle*, now withdrew, as if they were witnessing the work of a monstrous dragon. One by one, they left, looking back now and then to see if there was to be any fire or smoke.

"What's the matter?" Davy asked, innocently.

"I'll tell you what's the matter!" The big boy glared down at Davy who was too little to argue. "Do you want to know what's the matter?"

Davy nodded his head. Although he was rather frightened, he was glad that someone was consulting him.

"Boats are for water! That's what's the matter!" Then he turned and walked away, grumbling.

"He's right," said Jerry, wistfully. "Boats are for water."

"Yeah, boats are for water," echoed Davy, bravely.

"But there isn't any water," said Clem.

"Let me think," Marcus said. "Just give me a minute. I'll think of something." They all waited while he did some thinking.

Suddenly he cried, "I've got it!"

"Oh, Marcus, you're wonderful!" Clem clapped her hands.

"What?" Jerry asked, thinking that there was no end to Marcus's ideas.

"Now listen," he said with an air of mystery. "Just listen and stick with me. I know where there IS some water!"

Clem said, "You do?" with great curiosity and admiration. She trusted him completely.

"Where?" asked Jerry, not quite as trusting as Clem.

"Catfish Creek!" he replied.

Catfish Creek! There was a long silence. They knew what he meant. Every boy who had ever been raised in Chestnut Valley had at some time or other dreamed of sailing on Catfish Creek. There were gallons and gallons of water going to waste. The dreams of sailing or swimming never got any further than being dreams. There was a swift current and jagged rocks; moreover it was muddy and spoiled with trash that was thrown over the bridge or out of the factory. It couldn't even be used for fishing.

Marcus's idea was bold and a little frightening. But, now that it was spoken, it was also irresistible. If anyone but Marcus had made the suggestion, they would have scoffed and said, "Impossible!" But Marcus was brave and big and experienced; if they disagreed with him, they would seem young and cowardly. Besides, the idea was so enormous that they were already beginning to feel the trembling thrill of excitement.

8

CATFISH CREEK

"Well?" Marcus thought that they had had enough time to think about it.

"I suppose it wouldn't hurt to try it." Jerry's voice was low and crackly, as if it belonged to someone else.

"I guess my father wouldn't care," said Clem. She wouldn't have wanted Marcus to think that she was scared for anything in the world.

"I wonder if it'll float?" Jerry asked, more to himself than to the others.

"We can stay near the bank," Marcus said, "then if it sinks we can just jump out. There's nothing to worry about. I've been in lots of boats."

"Where?" Clem asked. She believed him but

she wanted to be very sure that they were doing the right thing.

"Oh, at camp . . . and things."

"What's the matter?" Davy asked suddenly, wondering why they were being so mysterious.

"We're going to make the boat move, little Davy," Clem replied.

Marcus looked at him and another idea flashed through his mind. "Davy can ride in the boat all the way to the Creek," he said. It was the first nice thing that he had said to Davy all day. If anyone suspected that he was bribing Davy to be quiet, it didn't show.

Davy was wild with excitement. They helped him up the ladder and when he was settled right in the middle of the *Lillybelle,* they put the ladder in beside him and began the journey to the creek bank.

On the surface it seemed like such an ordinary day, with such familiar sights all about them. There wasn't a soul out on the street; there was never a soul out on the street on hot summer afternoons. People were indoors, mostly. A few were in their backyards, sprinkling gardens or sleeping in hammocks. The air was still. The sky was a brilliant blue, with tracings of wispy clouds across it. The grass was green, with scorched tips. There was a sweet dusty smell all about.

Within, the children were shaking with excitement. They were going to do something that had never been done before.

When they reached the end of the street and were about to turn into Main Street, they turned the wagon wheels with their hands, to make sure that their precious load wouldn't be dumped. On they went, toward the bridge. They passed a man whom they didn't know. They passed a woman who was busy checking a shopping list. They passed one of their school friends who didn't even notice them. Then they saw Mr. Douglas, the policeman.

"Stop," Marcus said in a low voice. The procession stopped and the children huddled next to the *Lillybelle*, pretending to talk. If they didn't look at Mr. Douglas, perhaps he wouldn't look at them. Mr. Douglas looked up and down the street, wiped his forehead with his handker-chief, and went into the drugstore. It appeared that they had a good chance of reaching their destination without being stopped.

Then, suddenly, two boys who were even big-ger than Marcus appeared from nowhere. Charlie Bond and Arnold Busby, the two worst teasers in the whole town! They weren't really bad boys. They teased only when they didn't have anything to do. Well, this day they didn't have anything to do, so when they saw the *Lillybelle,* they stopped.

Charlie cried, "Where did you get THAT con-traption?"

"It's my father's," said Clem.

"Pretty neat. Where are you going with it?"

"Oh, not anywhere . . . very much," Jerry re-plied.

"Ho! What do you mean, not anywhere?"

"Just taking a walk," Marcus said, trying to keep cool.

His face began to twitch and his freckles looked like spots before the eyes when a flash camera

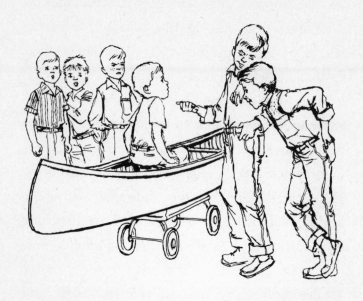

goes off. Clem watched him closely. In a way, she hoped that he would punch Charlie in the nose. But in another way, she hoped that he wouldn't because he might get punched back in the nose.

"Well," said Arnold, "maybe we'll just take a walk with you."

"No!" Clem cried out, fiercely.

"No!" said Charlie, imitating her high girl's voice. Then his voice went way down like a man's voice and he said, "Yes!"

"No!" shouted Davy from up in the *Lillybelle*.

Charlie looked up at the boat and began to laugh. "Look at the sailor boy!" He reached up to pull Davy out of the boat. Jerry was at his side instantly. Clem looked at Marcus frantically, waiting for him to come to Jerry's rescue. But Marcus was frozen to the spot.

Jerry was saying, "If you touch him, I'll kill you."

Charlie put his hands on his hips and roared with laughter.

"Wait a minute," Marcus said, at last. "Okay, if you want to walk with us, that's just fine."

Jerry and Clem stared at him, thinking that he had gone crazy with the heat. His frozen look was gone and in its place was a kind of smug look.

"Come on," he said and started to turn the wagon around. "Your father wants you to put the boat back in the garage, doesn't he, Clem?"

Clem, slightly confused, answered, "Yes . . . why yes, he does . . . I guess."

So they turned the wagon full around and began to walk back home.

In a very short while, Charlie and Arnold decided that this was a stupid, childish game and they wanted no part of it. Without a word, they peeled off from the formation and the children were once more alone.

"That was real smart, Marcus," Clem whispered. Her disappointment had vanished and he was her hero again.

As soon as they were sure that there would be no more intruders, they turned the wagon once more and continued with the adventure.

"Are you all right, little Davy?" Clem reached up and patted Davy's hand which was curled over the rim of the boat.

"Sure," he said. "Let's move!"

Marcus and Jerry picked up the ends of the rope. They were feeling safe again and also tender about girls and small children, after their close call.

The whole town seemed to be asleep. Even the clock over the bank on the square had stopped. The heat rose from the pavement and you could smell the hot tar that filled the cracks.

A car passed over the bridge; it rattled and vibrated.

Now this wasn't an ordinary little bridge, spanning an ordinary little stream. It was an enormous bridge that rose almost two stories high and it was about two stories down to the creek. The metal was rusty in spots where the weather had peeled away the paint. The planks on the sidewalk were creaky and they separated so that you could peek through them and see the water way down below under your feet. The children had walked over this bridge hundreds of times. Now it looked different, as if it were a person instead of a thing.

Grasping the rail that was about the height of their chins, they looked down into the water. It was a thick dirty gray. In the distance they could see the railroad trestle and beyond that the dam. There were huge rocks sticking out and clusters of scrawny shrubs growing along the banks.

They turned and looked at the creek in the other direction. There it became considerably wider. It made a sharp turn in the distance and

71

then disappeared. Large trees grew along that part of the bank. They had long willowy branches that dipped right down into the water.

The children looked in silence. It was like a vast cavern about to swallow them. They glanced at each other. This was their last chance to change their minds.

"Well, do you want to try it?" Marcus finally broke the silence.

"Sure," Jerry replied.

"Come on, let's go," Clem urged, fearing that she might lose her courage.

"Let's move!" called Davy.

They even looked at Major for approval. However, Major was quite unconcerned. As long as he was with them, he didn't care where they went.

They pulled the wagon over the bumpy planks, bumpety-bumpety-bumpety. When they crossed the bridge, they decided to go in the direction of the dam. They took the street running parallel to the creek. They passed the garage and heard the mechanic's hammer clanking on metal parts; they passed the tea room where people mostly drank coffee; they passed the laundry where steam hissed out of pipes; they passed the shoemaker's shop where a man stood in the window, his mouth full of tiny nails.

At last they stopped and Marcus said, "Let's try it here." They turned into a narrow path that led down to the Creek. It wasn't easy, but they managed to get the wagon down the slope without smashing it and the *Lillybelle* to pieces.

At the water's edge they lifted Davy down. They put the step ladder under a bush. Then carefully, they pulled the *Lillybelle* off the wagon and set her on the muddy bank.

The mud was thick and oily. The boat slid over the surface quite easily. Marcus and Jerry took off their sneakers and threw them into the boat. They waded out, gingerly feeling the bottom with their toes, and then they pulled the *Lillybelle* into the water.

First they persuaded Major to get in and lie down quietly. Then Clem and Davy got in and settled nervously on the floor.

Finally Marcus and Jerry got in. It was awkward holding the paddles and sitting down so they rested on their knees and prepared to paddle Indian style.

"All set?" Marcus asked, his voice curiously low.

"All set," replied Jerry.

"All set," gulped Clem.

Major was all set, too. His nose was on the floor and his paws were crossed over it. Davy's hands were clinging to his coat as if he expected them all to be jolted.

However, nothing happened. When the weight of all of them filled the *Lillybelle,* it sank into the mud and wouldn't budge. Before they even started they were stuck. Here they were, on water, where boats are supposed to be, and they still weren't moving.

9

THE *LILLYBELLE* IS LAUNCHED

Marcus and Jerry struggled with all their might, pushing against the mud with the paddles, but the *Lillybelle* still wouldn't budge.

Clem looked worried. "Won't it move?" she asked.

Marcus glanced sharply at her, thinking, "Why doesn't that girl stop asking questions, especially at a time like this!"

Davy slapped the sides of the boat and bounced around, impatiently. "Let's move!" he cried. "Let's go!"

Jerry was sweating and Marcus was grinding his teeth. Marcus got out and the boat began to rise ever so gently. Then Jerry got out and it continued to rise. They pushed her out until they were knee-deep in water. When they were cer-

75

tain that they were out of danger of getting stuck again, Marcus climbed in, pushed from behind by Jerry. He, in turn, hauled Jerry over the rim. With utmost care, they crawled along the bottom until they reached their proper places, Jerry in the bow and Marcus in the stern.

"We'll get it launched yet," Marcus said, grimly.

"Yes, I'm hungry," Davy looked alert. "Let's go where we're going so we can get back home for something to eat."

"I said 'launch,' not 'lunch.' "

"Oh," Davy said, wondering what in the world he had said that was wrong now.

He didn't have too much time to wonder for the boat was really and truly moving. They were moving and they were on water! That was what they had been waiting for since morning and now that it was so, they could scarcely believe it. Their bodies were tense and their faces solemn. The wonder of actually being on water made them silent and watchful.

Presently they felt a gentle swaying movement and they all began to relax. This was even nicer than they had imagined. It was so very exciting and there was nothing dangerous about it; it was as safe as sitting up in their own beds.

Marcus leaned over to dip his hand in the water. The *Lillybelle* leaned too. This gave them a small scare so they agreed that no one was to reach out, no matter how tempting it was.

Davy lifted his face happily, catching the tiny cooling breeze. He had released his grip on Major's coat. Even Major felt safe enough to raise his nose and sniff the new surroundings.

"Where are we going?" Clem asked. It seemed impossible for her NOT to ask questions.

"Let's go to Africa," Davy cried. He didn't know very many places and he had learned that one by now.

"No, let's go to China!"

"No, to Alaska!"

"No, to India!"

Marcus and Jerry dipped their paddles like veteran sailors. The trouble was that they were paddling against each other and they weren't about to go anywhere.

"I'm tired of all those old places," Marcus said. "Let's go somewhere new."

"Where?" Clem asked.

"Oh, I don't know. Let's discover a new place, a new island with lots of animals on it."

"Okay," Jerry agreed. "We can give it a name and give the animals names and maybe we can find some new people and give them names, too."

Davy was straining forward, trying to make the *Lillybelle* go faster. "Come on, come on, come on," he chanted.

The boat kept making little half-circles, first in one direction, then in the other. They certainly were not getting very far, toward either a real place or an imaginary one.

"How about Rapple-Dapple Island?" Jerry suggested.

"Or Boogle-Woogle Island? Or Pig-Dig Island?" Clem was having such a good time that she felt downright silly.

"No!" Marcus held up his hand, putting the paddle across his knees as he did so. "We have to have real words."

"But it's not a real place!"

"I don't care. The words have to be real. We

can call it Hot Dog Island or Hamburger Island . . ."

"I'm hungry!" cried Davy.

When Marcus stopped paddling, the *Lillybelle* suddenly and rather violently moved out to the middle of the stream. It was quite a surprise. The chatter stopped. Major jerked his head around to see what was happening. He sniffed as if he were smelling something unpleasant.

To be sure, the Creek did have an unpleasant smell. You didn't notice it when you were standing on the bridge, but here, right on top of the water, you couldn't get away from it. The children could see why it wasn't used for swimming. The water was muddy brown and there were patches of yellowish foam floating on the surface.

"Oooh! Dead fish!" exclaimed Clem, holding her nose.

"D-d-dead F-fish Island," Jerry said, trembling but not enough to miss the opportunity of naming the new place.

"There'll be some lizards and snakes . . ." Marcus offered.

Once the surprise of moving fast in deeper water was over, the chatter gradually picked up again.

"No!" Clem protested. "No snakes!"

"I want a panda," Davy cried.

"I want llamas and gnus." Jerry wished that someone would ask him to spell them. Unfortunately no one knew what they were. Marcus insisted that they have only real animals, not made-up ones. And Jerry insisted that llamas and gnus were as real as lizards and snakes, in some countries, that is.

"Oh," scoffed Marcus, "they're out of this world."

In fact, the children were, at this moment, out of this world. It was as if they had left the world that they knew so well, and by surrounding themselves with water, had gone into a new one. It was like being inside a bubble with nothing to think about except naming a new island.

Then suddenly, they were pulled back to the old world by Clem, who was screaming and pointing up toward the bridge.

"Look!"

They all looked. It was hard to believe but what they saw was an enormous crowd: the whole town, it seemed, standing on the bridge, looking down at them.

"What do you suppose they're doing there?" Clem asked.

This time Marcus didn't even hear her question. He had turned pale and was swallowing very hard.

"I bet Mom's up there," Davy yelled, with pride. He held up his face, as if he were having his picture taken. He waved and pointed to himself, not wanting to be missed.

"Ohhhh," Clem gave a low stomach-ache kind of groan as she recognized her mother by the pink dress that she was wearing. And her father was probably up there, too, wearing his white drugstore jacket. She had been saying "my father won't care" so often that she was beginning to believe it. Now, however, she knew that her father DID care about what she was doing. Unlike Davy, she tried to hide her face.

Jerry had his eyes fixed on Davy, the only one who wasn't concerned about what his parents were thinking. He had been given the responsibility of watching Davy and he had done a mighty poor job of it. He bit his lip and tried not to cry.

Marcus became frozen for the second time that day. It was true that he had made a deal with his mother. Neither of them had suspected that his day of freedom would lead him to this.

In an unguarded moment, the *Lillybelle* jerked and Marcus felt the paddle slide from his knees, into the water. He watched helplessly as it was caught up by the current and carried out of his reach. It went sailing down the creek all by itself.

10

HOW THEY LOOKED FROM THE BRIDGE

The crowd on the bridge had started with only one man. He had merely stopped to look down at the water, which was what people always did when they crossed the bridge. When he saw the children he simply couldn't believe his eyes. He stared and stared as if he were hypnotized. Presently, another man came along.

"What's up, Joe? You look as if you'd seen a ghost."

"Look!" Joe pointed to the *Lillybelle*. "I was watching those crazy kids down there. What do they think they're doing?"

"Where?" The second man was surprised. "Oh . . . now I see." He gave a long low whistle.

"I don't like the looks of it," Joe said.

"Don't worry. Kids always manage to take care of themselves."

"Maybe so, Norman . . . but . . ."

"They do the darnedest things. I remember when I was a kid. I always wanted to sail the old creek."

"Sure, you wanted to. But you never did it, did you?"

"No," Norman said, thoughtfully. "Come to think of it, I never did. I don't think anybody ever did . . . before today."

"There are some pretty big rocks out there. If those kids hit them, they're in trouble."

Norman scratched his head. "Maybe you're right. Maybe we'd better go down there."

As he was saying this, a third man joined them. "What in the world," he gasped, "are those kids doing down there?"

"That's what we're going to find out," replied Joe. He and Norman left, but not before several more people had gathered on the bridge.

"I wonder who they are?" someone asked. "I can't tell. All kids look alike to me."

"I don't know the children, but I recognize that dog," cried a lady. "That's Harry Stone's dog."

"If that's the Stones's dog, then the kids must be Jerry and Davy Stone."

"If that's Jerry and Davy, then I'm going to get their father. Harry Stone ought to know about this," said a man in the crowd.

As the man left, another man shouted, "The one with the red hair. I know him. That's the Cole boy. Yes, sir, that's Marcus Cole. I'm not surprised. He's always up to something."

"Oh, mercy!" groaned a woman. "The Coles are our neighbors. I'm going to get Mrs. Cole right away."

She pushed her way through the crowd and in a short while she returned, with Mrs. Cole panting at her heels. Mrs. Cole looked terrified. She hadn't bothered to take off her apron or comb her hair or put on her street shoes. She made her way to the railing and began to moan, "Oh, it's all my fault, it's all my fault. I shouldn't have made the deal with him, even for one day . . ."

Of course, the people standing near her didn't understand what she was saying. There were some consoling murmurs and assurances that every-thing would be all right. At this very moment there were some men on their way down to rescue the children. They kept telling her to take it easy.

Well, she was taking it easy all right. She was thinking, "Now Marcus Cole, if I've told you once, I've told you a hundred times not to go sailing on the creek . . ." But she HADN'T told him a hundred times not to go sailing on the creek. She hadn't told him even once. It had never occurred to her that he would ever do such a thing. "That boy is getting too big for his breeches," she mumbled to herself. "I'll fix him. He's not too big for a good old-fashioned spanking." However, she knew that she was not going to fix him, nor was she going to spank him. She knew that she was angry only because she was frightened. The only thing she wanted was for him to be safe. That was all.

In the meantime someone had recognized Clem. "That's the one with the funny short hair. She's a tomboy."

At this the lady from the beauty parlor, wearing her uniform, with combs sticking out of the pockets, pricked up her ears. "That's right!" she gasped. "I'd know her anywhere. She cut her own hair and I couldn't do a thing with it. That's Clem Robie, all right!"

A boy, standing nearby said, "Her mother's in the drugstore. I just saw her in there a few minutes ago. I'll go get her." He ran off to fetch Mrs. Robie.

When Mrs. Robie arrived, she took one long look at the children, grasped the rail and closed her eyes. People thought that she was going to faint. Several hands stretched out to catch her but she didn't faint. She mumbled, "No, no, no . . ."

The reason that she closed her eyes was to

recall her telephone conversation with Clem.

" . . . and we're having more fun and we're playing in that old boat of Daddy's and we're going to Africa in it . . ."

And she had answered, "Have a good time . . . and don't get wet," thinking that it was all a joke. And now she was mumbling, "No, no, no, Clem couldn't have meant that they were REALLY going to sail somewhere."

Now Mr. Stone pulled up in his pick-up truck. The crowd made way for him and he parked it right on the bridge. Ordinarily Mr. Stone was a law-abiding citizen who wouldn't have done this. But this was an emergency; traffic couldn't have passed over the bridge anyway because the crowd was so thick. Besides, Mr. Douglas, the policeman, was with him and escorted him right up to the railing.

"What can we do? How can we help?" several men spoke up. Everyone had such a feeling of helplessness.

"I don't know, yet," Mr. Douglas said. "We'll

have to figure out the best way of getting to them."

"Heavens! They're heading right for the rocks!" The worry on Mr. Stone's face showed in the paleness and in the way he was grinding his jaws.

In a few minutes Mrs. Stone, accompanied by Mrs. White, arrived on the scene. Mr. Stone put his arms around her to comfort her. She was trying not to cry. "I shouldn't have left them alone. I thought they'd be all right out in the barn."

"Now, don't blame yourself, dear," Mr. Stone said. "It could have happened with you in the house. I'm sure they had no idea of the seriousness of what they were doing."

Mr. Robie was the next one to arrive. He had been out of the store when the boy had come for Mrs. Robie and she had left him a note.

"What's the matter? What's happened?" he asked. His wife pointed to the children and he stared and grew pale. "If I'd known that this was to happen to the *Lillybelle* I never would have accepted her." He took his wife's hand and together they waited to see what would come of it.

The last of the parents to arrive was Mr. Cole. He knew what to expect because he had been told all along the way. It was almost a relief to be there and see it with his own eyes.

"That boy of mine!" he said fiercely. "I don't know what I'm going to do with him. I never did things like this when I was a kid."

"Now, Phil," spoke up an old man in the crowd, "I could tell you some stories about what you did when you were a kid. You've just forgotten."

"I suppose so," Mr. Cole replied. "I guess he's just at an age where he's got to do things big."

The time for looking and talking had long passed. It was the time for doing.

Mr. Douglas said, "We're not helping anything by being up here. Come on, let's go down."

He and the fathers and several other men started for the creek bank.

As they left, the excitement on the bridge grew more intense. The *Lillybelle* was being pulled

91

into the middle of the creek by the current and she was headed for the jagged rocks that were waiting for them just below the surface of the water.

A low solemn moan went up for Jerry dropped the other paddle and now the children had really lost control of the *Lillybelle*.

11

THE ROCKS

Jerry could scarcely believe that his paddle was gone. He hadn't been able to do much with it but it gave him some comfort just to hold it. Now it was gone. He stared at his hands as if he expected the paddle to jump out of the water and back into them. Then he saw that it was caught up by the current and was being swept downstream.

"I-I-I lost the paddle," he stammered, even though he knew that the others had seen it happen.

Marcus was facing Jerry. He said, "It's all right. Never mind. It's all right. Don't worry."

Jerry didn't believe him, but he was grateful

for Marcus's saying something helpful, for once.

"I want to go home!" Davy began to wail.

"Now don't worry, don't worry. It's all right, It's all right. Just hang on, hang on . . ." Jerry was shouting at the top of his voice. The wind kept blowing his hair into his eyes. He brushed it away with one hand and tried to hang on with the other.

"Stop saying things twice, stop saying things twice," Clem screamed, hanging on to the sides of the *Lillybelle*.

They could see little eddies all around them; they became more powerful as they drew nearer the rocks. They had heard people talk of the rocks in the creek and now they were beginning to realize why people had said that they were treacherous. You couldn't see them for they were beneath the surface of the water. And the water was so murky that it made them invisible.

Major put his nose under his paws again. He looked bewildered and frightened. His entire body was trembling the way a dog's body trembles when there is a thunderstorm.

"J-J-J-Jerry, can you swim?" Clem asked, her teeth chattering.

"Sh-sh-sh-ure I can," Jerry replied. Jerry was indeed a good swimmer but he looked miserable at the thought of swimming in this dirty water with dead fish floating by.

"I c-c-c-can't swim," Clem cried.

"Don't worry, if we tip over hang on to Major. He's a good swimmer."

Clem looked ruefully at Major, who looked as if he couldn't save a flea.

The stern of the *Lillybelle* was bobbing around as if it couldn't decide what to do. Jerry, sitting in the bow, looked down and saw that the boat had stopped moving. They were caught upon the rocks and stuck there. The stern was left dangling. It made little slap-slap noises, as if it were trying to struggle out of a trap.

Davy's face which was usually pink and white was now a light green. He put his head down next to Major. "Oh," he groaned, "oh, I'm dizzy."

"Lie down flat," Jerry said. "Lie down flat and don't move."

Davy willingly obeyed.

Jerry ran his hand around the inside of the shell of the boat. He wondered if the rocks had poked a hole through the canvas. As far as he could feel it was still safe and sturdy. He didn't know how long that would be.

Marcus wasn't saying a word. His face had not only a peculiar color but also a peculiar expression. He was staring at Clem's back, almost as if he couldn't bear to look into the water. His lips were moving but no words were coming from them.

"D-D-Davy, can you swim?" Clem asked. "C-can you, Davy? Can you swim?"

"Sure," Davy lifted his head for a moment. "Sure I can swim. Boy, am I dizzy!"

The people on the bridge were now waving and shouting all kinds of things that were lost in the air.

Men began appearing on the bank. They too were shouting but it was impossible to understand a thing that they were saying. All that the children could make out was, "Sit still! Sit still! !"

Jerry and Marcus, who were on their knees, sank to the bottom of the boat. It felt safer that way. They could do nothing but wait and hope that the *Lillybelle* would work its way free from the rocks. A few birds flew overhead. They were small and harmless but they looked like enormous vultures to the children. The smell became worse and soon, not only Davy, but all the children felt sick.

The men had spread out all along the bank; some opposite the boat, some under the bridge, and others on the other side of the bridge. They were taking off their shoes and socks and were preparing to wade into the creek.

Clem, still holding the sides of the boat, turned around to look at Marcus. "C-c-can you swim? Can you, Marcus? Can you swim?" she asked.

Marcus was looking hopefully toward the men on the bank. He was especially looking for his father. He didn't even hear Clem.

"Sit still!" Jerry shouted.

He was sitting right on top of those ugly rocks. The powerful little eddies made the boat go up-down, up-down, up-down, with slapping sounds.

The men on the bank were coming into the water now. Mr. Stone was ahead of the others. He was coming slowly for the current was swift and it was difficult to stand upright. Besides, the bed of the stream was not very comfortable for bare feet. Now he was waist deep in water.

Not far behind him came Mr. Robie and Mr. Cole. All the men had removed their shirts and Mr. Cole had left his glasses on the bank.

In the distance the children heard the siren of the town fire engine. At first they thought that there was a fire somewhere, but then they realized that everyone, even the fire department, was on hand to take part in their rescue. This would have been exciting under any other circumstances. But sitting on top of the rocks in the middle of Catfish Creek, waiting for the *Lillybelle* to be dashed to pieces, was only terrifying.

Now Mr. Stone was shoulder deep in the water. He was about to plunge in and swim the rest of the way. The men were close enough to talk to the children.

"Sit very still," Mr. Stone shouted.

"If she tips, hang on to the boat," yelled Mr. Robie.

A short distance behind, Mr. Cole cupped his hands and called, "Don't move. We're getting there!"

Davy was still flat in the bottom of the boat. Marcus and Jerry sat very still as they had been told, but Clem, hearing her father's voice, cried, "Daddy! Daddy!" and tried to stand up.

"Sit down!" Jerry screamed as the boat began to tip.

Marcus reached over and pulled her down and held her tightly. She tried to jerk away from his grasp but he held on until she became calm.

All of this movement changed the position of the boat on the rocks. It made a crunching sound, then another, and another.

Mr. Stone was swimming toward them. He was very near, only a few feet away. He was just about to reach out and seize the rim of the *Lillybelle* when she came loose and was caught up by the current. He just missed catching hold of it. In a few wild moments the *Lillybelle* tossed crazily, made a complete circle, and then was carried downstream.

12

DOWNSTREAM VOYAGE

As soon as the *Lillybelle* was caught in the current she went downstream as fast as if she had a motor. Boats are supposed to move and boats are for water! Perhaps so, but it would have been much more comfortable dreaming of Africa in Clem Robie's backyard.

Clem screamed and lay down on top of Davy who was lying on top of Major. Marcus, with his legs up in the air, slid down so that he was now lying on his back. Jerry, with his hands in the air, slid down so that he was now lying on his stomach.

The men along the shoreline and the people on the bridge were staring frozenly at the children. They were utterly helpless to do anything. They saw the boat running away with four children and a dog and could do nothing but watch and wait.

Now the *Lillybelle* was almost directly beneath the bridge and they could see the mass of faces, arms, legs, and paws, all tangled together in a heap.

As the boat passed under the bridge, the people stooped and peered between the cracks in the wooden planks. There were sounds that weren't like real words, but gasps and moans and even some sighs.

Then the *Lillybelle* passed to the other side of the bridge. The people, like a great wave, shifted to the other side, almost as if the bridge had been tipped and they were all sliding with it.

On the other side of the bridge, the creek began to widen considerably and there were fewer rocks. The *Lillybelle* seemed to slow down; at least it seemed to be more steady. One by one, the heads lifted. Clinging to the sides, the children pulled themselves up so that only their noses were showing. They looked at the water and saw a curious assortment of things floating by: dead fish, branches, gum wrappers, strange insects, and yellowish scum. What a sight!

"I wish I could swim," Clem managed to whisper. Her face was streaked with mud and tears and her chopped hair was standing out in all directions, like broken toothpicks.

"Let's go home now," Davy cried, mournfully. It was the first time that his face had been out of Major's coat.

Jerry pulled himself to his knees and looked at the passing scenery. "We must have been going five hundred miles an hour," he said solemnly, and they all agreed that it must have been at least that.

They looked back and saw the men running along the shore, trying to catch up with them. At the rate they were going it was a losing race, and the children felt a loneliness because they were cut off and didn't know what would happen next. They were so very tired.

"I wish I were home," Clem said, wistfully.

Davy said, "I do, too. I'm hungry."

The color was beginning to come back to Davy's face. His hands still clung to Major. Major had stopped trembling but his paws still covered his nose and his eyes looked as if they were asking when all this sailing nonsense would be over.

Marcus was the only one who had not spoken.

Jerry looked at him and asked quietly, "Where do you suppose we're going?"

Marcus shook his head without replying.

"What'll we do?" Clem asked, and then she added, "You're the captain. What'll we do?"

Something that sounded like a sob stuck in Marcus's throat and he shook his head again.

Jerry looked at Marcus curiously and trying to smile, said, "I guess were're going wherever the creek goes. I guess. I guess it goes . . . down to the lake."

"Oh, no!" Clem cried. "I don't want to go to the lake. That's about a thousand miles away. I want to go home!"

The bridge and the people on it were getting

smaller and smaller. As soon as they went around the bend the bridge would be out of sight. It was like leaving their world behind.

What would it be like to be carried out to the lake? It would be like getting swept into the ocean where you would be just a tiny speck and no one would ever find you.

The men running along the bank were getting smaller too. And they too would disappear as soon as the *Lillybelle* passed the bend in the creek.

Here it was, that mysterious bend. The children used to wonder what happened to the creek after it turned the corner. To them it was a place where the sun settled down for the night and made the creek look beautiful. It was a place where the huge trees dipped into the water and fringed it with the sunset colors of yellow and gold. It was a place where rainbows might be born or daydreams might end.

In a few minutes they would see it with their own eyes. It was exciting even though it might carry them away forever and ever.

Jerry craned his neck to see what was ahead. Then he looked at Marcus and asked, "What'll we do?"

They had always asked Marcus what to do, and Marcus had always told them.

Clem, her eyes wide with curiosity and excitement and fear, called back over her shoulder to Marcus. "What WILL we do, Marcus?" she demanded.

And Marcus kept his silence. Suddenly he folded his arms over his knees and put his head down on his arms and cried. Marcus Cole was crying. Marcus Cole, who had made a grown-up deal with his mother, Marcus who gave the orders because he was the biggest and the oldest, Marcus who was the captain of the *Lillybelle*.

Clem glanced at Jerry. She didn't know what to make of Marcus's behavior. She was sad and disappointed. How could she ever again believe in him or feel supported by his strength?

Jerry looked away. He was somewhat embarrassed; but even more he felt such a deep hurt for Marcus that it was almost as painful as if it

were happening to himself. He thought that he'd better get into a position to take over in case there needed to be any taking-over. Very carefully he turned his body around so that he was now looking out over the bow. In this position, not only could he see what was happening ahead, but also, he wouldn't have to look at Marcus and intrude upon his privacy.

As they approached the curve, the current seemed to make a sharp shift. It was certainly going to hit the bank. And, of course where the current went, there would go the *Lillybelle*.

However, instead of hitting the bank, the current curved along with it, and the children found themselves, not in the middle of the creek, but quite close to the bank. If they had been able to stop, they could have reached out and touched it. They did, in fact, touch some of the branches that were trailing in the water. Just doing this took away some of the terrible feeling of isolation that had come over them.

A few minutes ago they had been huddled in the bottom of the boat. Now they were all sitting up straight, alert and eager to see what would happen next.

Right up ahead was something that appeared to be land but was not a part of the bank. Then, as they came nearer, they realized that it was a tiny island, right in the middle of Catfish Creek. It was hard to believe but there it was, no bigger than their backyards, but a real island, a body of land completely surrounded by water.

They had wanted to discover a new island and here it was. What were those new-island names? Boogle-Woogle? Digaramoo? Hot Dog Island? Hamburger Island? Dead Fish Island?

Whatever the name, it looked beautiful to the children. They wanted to stop and explore it, but there was one big problem. They didn't know how to stop. They saw that it was indeed quite close to the bank, almost as if it had once been a part of it and had been sliced off by the water.

There were two big trees and a great deal of low underbrush growing on the island. They were the same kind of willowy trees that grew on the bank, trees that dipped into the water.

Jerry, on his knees, leaned forward. Suddenly he shouted, "Grab the branches! Grab the branches!"

The others took up the cry, "Grab the branches!" and eagerly held out their hands. Just as they passed the nearest tree on the island, they grabbed the branches and the *Lillybelle* stopped with an enormous jolt!

13

THE ISLAND

Jerry was almost pulled out of the *Lillybelle* by the great impact. He wound his fingers around the slender leafy branches and held on as hard as he could even though his hands hurt from the cuts that they made. He dug his knees into the bottom of the boat to keep his balance.

Davy was too small to catch the branches. He dived into Major's coat again and hid his face from whatever new crisis was waiting for them.

Clem's thin body looked hardly bigger than the branches which she grasped. She was pretty strong for a girl. She hugged the branches to her and closed her eyes and hung on ferociously.

Marcus, aroused out of his sadness and shame,

almost missed the branches by flaying his arms too wildly, but soon he too caught them and hung on for dear life.

Their position now was an exceedingly delicate one, even more delicate than when they were on the rocks. For now the current was pushing the boat onward and the branches, anchored by the children's bodies, were holding it back. It was like being suspended in the air.

The children and the boat were right in the middle of this battle between the current and the branches. They were afraid of letting loose of the branches, fearing the boat would be swept out from under them. If only the *Lillybelle* had run onto the island. If only they could get out of the current, they could climb out of the *Lilly-belle* and wade to the island. If only they were sure enough of themselves to swing on the branches over to the island. If, if, if . . .

"Hang on!" Jerry said, his teeth chattering again. He couldn't count how many times his teeth chattered that day.

"Oh, don't worry!" Clem replied. She wouldn't

have let go for anything. Even if the boat had been carried away, she would have hung on.

"They're coming," Marcus said. "I can hear them shouting. They're coming. We HAVE to hang on till they get here." It was the first time that Marcus had spoken. They were strangely glad to hear his voice.

He was right. Soon the others could hear the voices of the men coming around the bend. There was nothing to do now but to wait. If only they were strong enough to keep their holds on the branches until the rescuers arrived.

While they were waiting Davy lifted his head once more and looked around.

"Look!" he said, pointing to the island.

"It's an island, little Davy," said Clem. "Don't be afraid. Your daddy will be here soon."

Davy wasn't especially afraid. He said, with his usual innocent curiosity, "Is this Africa?"

The others had to laugh in spite of themselves. They had been sure that they would never be able to laugh again, but there they were, laughing at death's door.

"I'm afraid it isn't," Marcus said, without his usual sharp tone when speaking to Davy. "It's still plain ol' Chestnut Valley."

"Look!" Davy cried again.

"It's—it's an island," Clem repeated. "It's an island I said."

"I don't mean the eye-lind," Davy said. "I mean that!"

The children turned their heads as much as they could without loosening their hold. Davy was pointing to an object on the island. It was half buried in the mud. But it was colorful so that the part that was showing could be plainly seen.

"What is it, Davy?" Jerry asked.

"I—I don't know," Davy said. Suddenly he stopped pointing and looked for something else.

But it was too late. Jerry had seen the object already. He was so startled that he almost lost his grip on the branches.

"How did THAT get here!" He exclaimed.

"I don't know," Davy said.

Jerry was too uncomfortable to press Davy any

further about the object. His arms were aching and his hands were being cut by the branches. He tried to shift the weight to his shoulders by leaning against the branches but he found that his shoulders ached too.

"What is it?" Clem asked. She was so full of curiosity that even her discomfort didn't stop her from asking.

"My mother's Mexican shopping basket," Jerry replied.

"But how did it get HERE?" Clem was so curious that she almost forgot their danger.

"Ask him," Jerry said.

"How DID it, Davy?"

"I don't know." Davy wasn't going to get cornered into unpleasant conversations with anyone, so he pressed his face against Major and moaned, "Oh, I'm dizzy again."

"Lie down." Jerry advised, patiently. He knew Davy well enough to recognize when he was putting on an act.

It was getting more and more difficult to hang on to the branches. They were so exhausted that

114

they didn't know if their strength would hold until the men arrived. The boat was moving under them in fierce zig-zags, as if it were trying to get away from them.

The men were getting closer. They too were exhausted from having run so far; and they were frightened of what they might find when they got there. Far in the distance the children could hear the sound of the fire siren again, louder and louder with each passing moment. And each passing moment seemed like years and years.

At last the men reached the bank opposite the *Lillybelle*. They took one glance at the strange sight of the children clinging to the willowy limbs arching over the water and they knew they must hurry or it would be too late.

"Hang on!" they shouted just as they had shouted, "Sit still!" when the boat was on the rocks. "Hang on, we're coming! Hang on! Don't let go!"

"We're hanging on," Jerry shouted back. He was puffing from hanging on, as well as from worry and fatigue.

"Daddy, Daddy, hurry!" Clem cried.

"Come get me, Daddy!" Davy called.

"Hurry!" Marcus urged. He could feel the branches slipping. Either he would have to let go soon or the branch would pull him right up, out of the boat.

The men were entering the water again. It wasn't very far but they would have to get through the strong current. Even though they were big and strong that would be difficult, especially since they had used so much strength in running.

As the children grew weaker, it seemed that the *Lillybelle* was more determined to get away from them. She bounced and strained over the wild current. This sapped even more of the children's strength. Suddenly Clem looked at her hands and saw that they were bleeding. This was too much for her. She let go of the branches and slumped forward in the boat.

Marcus, alarmed by seeing Clem in a heap beside him, reached out and his branches snapped out of his hands. Jerry was left holding the boat

116

all by himself. It was too much. The *Lillybelle*, with one great heave, tipped over and the children were sent scrambling into the current.

14

THE STRUGGLE

The *Lillybelle,* suddenly free, went hurtling and bumping downstream with the current, to be lost forever and ever. The men looked on helplessly, unable to move or even to cry out. For a few moments that seemed like years, they were so terrified that they were frozen in their positions.

Davy was still clinging to Major's coat. His hands gripped the fur so hard that Major was unable to move without him. The water rolled over them. Major fought the current, and ever so gradually he managed to move to the island. If he had been alone it would have been easy for him, but with Davy on his back he had to work especially hard. Davy closed his eyes and kept spitting out the water. At last, with super effort, they reached the island. They crawled up to the dry land and both rolled over and lay down and panted.

Jerry was still clinging to the branches. He bounced up and down, in and out of the water, like a fish at the end of a pole. If only he could get the branches to swing, he could get clear of the menacing current and jump onto the island. But he didn't have enough remaining strength to swing, only enough barely to hang on.

For a fleeting second the thought that even hanging on would no longer be possible. Then he heard his father's voice cry, "Hang on, boy." He had heard his father's voice say that a million times before when he had needed comfort or support, "Take it easy, boy," or "Hit the ball, boy," or "Count ten, boy." Hearing the "Hang on, boy" gave him an extra amount of magic courage and he did just that. He hung on.

In the meantime Marcus was floundering around in the current, trying desperately to keep his head above water. He had never answered Clem's question about his being able to swim. Now it was plain to be seen that he was an excellent swimmer. He was trying to reach the island, but in order to do so he had to swim against the current. He swam ahead a foot and was swept back two feet, forward, backward, forward, backward. He couldn't keep this up forever. Either he would have to make it soon or he would be swept downstream after the *Lillybelle*.

At one point he found himself almost under Jerry. He tried to reach Jerry's branch. He made an enormous effort and gave a lurch to seize it. However, Jerry's feet were in the way. If he had seized those dangling feet, he probably would have pulled Jerry down into the water with him.

Jerry looked down and saw what Marcus was trying to do. He pulled himself higher onto the branch to make room for him but Marcus was unable to grasp it. He needed both arms to fight the current.

However, the weight of Jerry moving up on the branch set it swinging a little. He pumped his body, as if he were on a swing, and made it sway a little more. Suddenly there was a great crunch and the branch split and swung in toward the island like falling timber. Jerry was deposited on dry land, not far from where Major and Davy were catching their breath. He let go and sagged gratefully to the earth and lay very still.

Marcus thrashed around desperately. He was being carried farther and farther downstream. He was almost ready to give up when he felt another body next to his and saw his father. He felt himself being hoisted to his father's shoulder. He lay his head on the back of his father's neck.

"Can you hang on to me?" his father was saying.

He answered by winding his arms more firmly.

"Good boy!" his father said.

There was a thick rope tied around Mr. Cole's waist. The other end of the rope was being held by some of the men on the shore. When they saw Marcus was secure on his father's back, they pulled and brought them both safely out of the current.

As soon as they reached the bank, they rolled Marcus onto his stomach and pumped some water out of him by using artificial respiration.

The fire engine was pulling up to the scene. It had plowed through an empty field because there was no road and now the firemen were jumping out from all sides, ready to go into action.

The men picked Marcus up from the ground and carefully put him on the back of the fire truck. Then they wrapped him in warm thick blankets.

Marcus was more frightened than hurt. In a few minutes he was sitting up, blinking and watching the men. He wasn't quite sure what had happened or where the other children were. He didn't even know whether they were safe or not.

His father was sitting beside him. When he sat up his father said, "Are you all right? Better lie down for a while."

"I'm fine. I'm okay. But . . ."

"But what?" Mr. Cole tried to hold him down.

"Where's Jerry?"

"He's okay. He's over there," Mr. Cole said pointing to the island where Marcus could see Jerry.

"And Davy . . .?" he asked.

"He's over there, too. See him with Major?"

"Oh, yes." Marcus saw them and a faint smile passed over his face.

But something was wrong. Someone was missing. There was no smile on his father's face. He looked grim and tense.

Suddenly Marcus pushed his father aside, threw off the blankets, and jumped off the fire truck.

"Clem!" Marcus screamed at the top of his voice.

Clem was the only one still in the water. No one knew where she was. No one had seen her.

Before anyone could stop him, Marcus was in the water again, wading out toward the current.

15

CLEM

"Come back, Marcus!"

"Marcus, the men will find her!"

"Marcus, you don't know where to look!"

"Her father is out there! He'll get her!"

But Marcus kept on going. He didn't even hear the shouts around him. He HAD to find Clem! He WOULD find her! He had acted in a cowardly way in the boat and he COULDN'T let her die believing him to be a coward. Besides . . . besides, Clem was wonderful and he was more fond of her than anyone he knew, almost, and he simply HAD to find her.

And he remembered how terrified Clem had been because she didn't know how to swim, and he had been annoyed because she asked so many questions.

"Clem can't swim," he said, mostly to himself. Then, louder, he called, "Clem can't swim." And, finally fully understanding her fear he shrieked, "CLEM CAN'T SWIM! She can't swim. She can't swim!" And he ran stumbling through the water.

Over on the island Jerry and Davy were watching intently. Mr. Stone had managed to reach the island and the three waited. They waited for everyone to be counted and then they, too, realized that Clem was missing.

"Clem," Jerry whispered softly. When he saw Marcus jump into the water, he whispered, "Marcus!" He began to shake and Mr. Stone put a comforting arm around him.

"No matter what happens, you stay here with Davy."

Mr. Stone went to the edge of the water and prepared to jump in if Marcus should get into trouble again.

Major walked around the island nervously, sniffing and digging and grovelling in the dirt.

He kept returning to Davy's side, back and forth. If Davy moved but an inch, Major was beside him instantly.

The men on the bank were spreading out again. They sent several strong swimmers out to help Mr. Robie who had been in the water from the moment that the *Lillybelle* was tipped. His head could be seen bobbing around but he was getting exhausted. The fresh swimmers took hold of him and dragged him on to the island. Then Mr. Stone held him while the others continued the search.

"Clem! Clem!" Mr. Robie groaned, "Clem, Clem, Clem . . ."

"You must rest a bit," Mr. Stone said. "They're doing everything that can possibly be done."

Major was barking now. His bark had an eerie quality, like dogs baying at the moon. Even though the others were in no mood to explore the island, he wasn't going to miss the opportunity. He dug up bits of debris that had been washed up and he barked with each new discovery.

Now Major dug up Mrs. Stone's Mexican basket at the spot where Davy had pointed. He carried it over to Jerry who took it from him sadly. He was no longer curious about how it had come to be there. All the fun of finding things was gone. Then Major went all the way out to the tip of the island where it was worn by the action of the water. He barked and barked. At first no one listened to him, but after a while the noise made them uneasy. He tried to get Davy to come with him but Davy was held fast by Jerry's hand.

Marcus was right back in the center of the current. His father was right behind him. However, this time, instead of fighting the current, Marcus let himself go along with it. He was being bruised and battered and carried downstream but it was easier than fighting it. Down, down, down he went to the very tip of the island. He saw Major and heard him bark.

"That crazy dog!" he muttered. "He just doesn't know. He doesn't know what's happened."

Then suddenly he saw why Major was barking. He saw what the others back there couldn't see.

He saw Clem. There she was, dangling in the water and clinging desperately to a clump of bushes on the island. Her wet, chopped hair made her look like a drowned rat. She had been washed up there and was holding on fiercely, too weak to call for help.

Marcus realized that the current would take him right to the spot. When he reached her he put one arm around her waist to hold her up and with the other arm he seized another sturdy clump of bushes. He waited for a few moments to catch his breath. He could smell the strong scent of peppermint leaves that grew thick and wild.

By this time Mr. Robie had reached the spot. He pulled first Clem and then Marcus out of the water. And it was none too soon, for the clump to which Clem had been clinging had been weakened by her weight and it suddenly pulled out of the ground and went plunging into the water.

Clem and Marcus lay on the ground, dazed and worn.

Presently Marcus whispered, "Are you all right?"

"Is that you, Marcus?" she asked. Even at a time like this, Clem had to ask a question.

This time, however, instead of being annoyed, Marcus smiled and said, "Sure! Who'd you think it was!"

Suddenly her eyes opened very wide. She exclaimed, "You saved me! Marcus, you saved my life!"

Marcus became embarrassed and tried to think of something to say that wouldn't sound silly. But he didn't have to say anything. Mr. Cole and Jerry and Davy were upon them and no one said anything.

There they were, all together again: Marcus, Jerry, Davy, Clem, and Major. They stared at each other. It was as if they were counting to make sure that they were all there.

Then a curious thing happened. Instead of jumping with joy, instead of embracing each other in pure relief, instead of laughing and shouting at being alive and well, they all began to cry. Such howls of sobbing that went up all over the island! Such boo-hooing that reached the ears of the startled men on the bank!

"Now . . . what's the matter?" asked Mr. Stone, bewildered. "Everyone's safe and we're going home."

"I'm just hap-p-py," cried Jerry.

"Me, too," echoed Davy.

"I'm so ti--red," groaned Marcus.

"Blub-blub-blub," was all that Clem could say.

"Is 'blub-blub-blub' all you can say at a time like this?" Mr. Robie was indeed puzzled.

And Clem's only reply was, "Blub-blub-blub!"

Well, by this time the firemen had rigged up all sorts of ladders and the children and Major were carried over to the bank. They were wrapped in blankets and lifted up to the back of the fire truck. Everyone was ready to move again. This time to the most welcome sight of home. And it was high time, for the sun was just beginning to dip into that mysterious spot in the bend of the creek. Only it wasn't mysterious any longer.

16

HOME AGAIN

Clem went to bed very early that night. Ordinarily she bounded up the steps, three at a time, but that night she went up like a lady, her father leading the way and her mother guiding her arm. She took a hot bath and climbed into her soft cozy bed. Then her mother brought her a tray with hot soup, hot milk, and hot buttered toast. It was the best food that she had ever tasted.

It was the first time in Clem's life that she thought it was wonderful simply to be in her own house and in her own bed. When they had entered the house, her father's clothes were still wet and so were hers. She had looked fondly at things as if she were seeing them for the first time: little things like the clock on the mantel that was pretty but wouldn't go; the arrangement of the furniture; the umbrella stand; the wall-paper patterns. They were all as familiar as her own self and yet, they were different.

Clem wanted to talk a little before going to sleep, so her mother and father pulled chairs up to her bed and they let her talk.

"I'm sorry . . ." she came around to saying at last.

"Sorry?" her father asked. He was constantly perplexed about the ways of little girls.

"About losing your boat," she said.

"Now, now, you forget about that. We've never used the boat and chances are we never would use it."

"We didn't really mean to do what we did, when we started. I mean. I mean, well . . . you know what I mean."

"Yes, dear," Mrs. Robie patted and smoothed the blankets. "We know what you mean. We're just thankful that you're safe. That's all that counts now."

"I think I've changed, Mother. I feel sort of
. . . different."

What Clem was feeling and didn't know how
to express was that she didn't think she'd have
to wear boy's clothes or chop off her hair or play
rough games anymore. She felt like a girl now
and that's the way she wanted it to be. She didn't
think that she'd ever have that awful loneliness
again. . .

Suddenly she looked at her mother and asked,
"Mother, am I pretty?"

"You're very pretty, dear," her mother replied.

And that was Clem's last question for the day.
In a few minutes she was sound asleep.

Jerry and Davy Stone were also doing something for the first time. They were taking a bath
without being told. After having been in cold
unfriendly water, it was nice to be in warm
friendly water.

Bed would be early that night so they were
permitted to have supper in their pajamas. Jerry
was very quiet at the table. He was so sleepy

that he could scarcely keep his eyes open.

Davy, on the other hand, was chattering like a parrot. He ate very fast and between mouthfuls gave a running description of the voyage. How it felt to be out there in the middle of the creek. How he had been a very important member of the crew. How he would have run things if he had been the captain.

Mrs. Stone let him chatter for a while, then asked, in a very business-like tone, "Now, tell me, how did it get there?"

There was a sudden silence in the room. Jerry became bright and Davy became sleepy.

"Well?" Mrs. Stone was waiting.

"What do you mean?" Davy asked, innocently.

"I think you know what I mean."

"May I have some more potatoes, please?"

"Certainly. Now! You found the Mexican basket on the island. HOW did it get there?"

"Well . . ." Davy began, taking a deep breath.

"Well WHAT?" Jerry couldn't control his curiosity.

"Well, one day, I borrowed it . . ."

"Ye-s?" Mrs. Stone was still waiting.

"To take to school . . ."

"Ye-s?"

"For SHOW AND TELL."

"Ye-s?"

"When I got to the bridge I wanted to see how far I could reach . . . and I dropped it . . . someone pushed me."

"Of course," said Mrs. Stone, "but why didn't you tell me this before? All these weeks I've been asking you to look for the basket and you acted as if you didn't know a thing about it. Honey, it's always much easier to tell the truth in the first place."

"You never asked me if I knew where it was," Davy said. "You always just asked me to look for it. And you never asked me if I dropped it in the creek."

Jerry looked at Mrs. Stone. Mrs. Stone looked at Mr. Stone and Mr. Stone pretended to look for something under the table.

"Well," Mrs. Stone concluded, "enough adventure, enough *Lillybelle*, and enough talking. Up to bed with you. Tomorrow is another day."

"Amen!" agreed Mr. Stone as he smiled and lit his pipe.

In the meantime, Marcus had also discovered something new. He discovered that he had been rude, not because he wanted to be rude but because it had become a habit. He had thought that it made him seem grown up.

He didn't especially feel like being grown-up right now. He was happy to be told what to do and to have his parents fuss over him. But somewhere inside, something was sticking him, like a pin. He wanted very much to get rid of whatever it was.

"I'm sorry to have caused so much trouble," he finally managed to say.

"Let's forget about it now," his mother said. "It's all over now and thank goodness, the ending was a happy one."

"But it might not have been . . ." Marcus insisted, "and it was all my fault . . ."

"Now, now, it's all over, Marcus." Mrs. Cole

138

tried to make him forget it, but Mr. Cole signalled her by shaking his head. He thought that Marcus should talk about it if he wanted to and get it out of his system.

"You did a fine thing, son," Mr. Cole said. "Clem will never forget what you did. Never."

Marcus smiled. "Clem's pretty nice . . . for a girl, that is."

Then he began to yawn and agreed that it wasn't too early for an eleven-year old to go to bed, considering what the day had been.

"Oh, by the way, Mom, do you mind if I put Boodle in the kitchen for the night? It gets kind of chilly out on the porch."

"Of course not," Mrs. Cole replied. "You put him anywhere you like."

For a moment they could both hear her words, "If I've told you once, I've told you a hundred times . . ." and they both smiled at the unspoken joke.

Then Marcus went up to his room and saw the toys that he had scattered on the floor that very morning. It seemed like a thousand years ago.

He felt so good that he decided to pick them up, here and now, and never scatter them again. But his muscles were sore and his bones ached. One more day wouldn't matter.

He climbed into bed and thought that if he lived to be five thousand years old, nothing would ever feel so warm and good as his bed felt at that moment. He turned out the light and saw the moonlight on the floor. He watched the curtain flutter at the window. He had never noticed it before, but that fluttering made a nice rhythmic pattern. In a few moments it lulled him to sleep.

The End